A Kooties Club MYSTERY

Membership Card

Name

Nickname

School

Age

Permission is granted by the publisher to reproduce the Kooties Club Membership Card.

The Mystery of Ben Franklin's Ghost

by M. J. Cosson

Perfection Learning® CA

Cover and Inside Illustrations: Michael A. Aspengren

For information, contact
Perfection Learning® Corporation,
1000 North Second Avenue, P.O. Box 500,
Logan, Iowa 51546-1099.
Tel: 800-831-4190 • Fax: 712-644-2392
Paperback 0-7891-2394-0
Cover Craft® 0-7807-7746-8

6 7 8 9 10 PP 08 07 06 05 04 03

Table of Contents

Introduction

Abe, Ben, Gabe, Toby, and Ty live
in a large city. There isn't much for
kids to do. There isn't even a park
close by.

Their neighborhood is made up of
apartment houses and trailer parks.
Gas stations and small shops stand
where the parks and grass used to be.
And there aren't many houses with
big yards.

Ty and Abe live in an apartment complex. Next door is a large vacant lot. It is full of brush, weeds, and trash. A path runs across the lot. On the other side is a trailer park. Ben and Toby live there.

Across the street from the trailer park is a big gray house. Gabe lives in the top apartment of the house.

The five boys have known each other since they started school. But they haven't always been friends.

The other kids say the boys have cooties. And the other kids won't touch them with a ten-foot pole. So Abe, Ben, Gabe, Toby, and Ty have formed their own club. They call it the Kooties Club.

Here's how to join. If no one else will have anything to do with you, you're in.

The boys call themselves the Koots for short. Ben's grandma calls his grandpa an *old coot*. And Ben thinks his grandpa is pretty cool. So if he's an old coot, Ben and his friends must be young koots.

The Koots play ball and hang out with each other. But most of all, they look for mysteries to solve.

Chapter 1

Ben's New Neighbor

"I'm too young for all this homework," said Ben.

"Me too," agreed Toby. "I wish I'd kept my big mouth shut. Now Miss Klug wants me to enter the science fair."

"At least you don't have to give a report," Ben said. "You don't have to stand in front of the whole class."

Ben and Toby were walking home from school. Their class was learning about the early days of the United States. They were learning about the

men who wrote the Declaration of Independence.

Ben and Toby just wanted to forget about school for a few hours. It was time to play. But they both had homework. They neared Ben's trailer.

"What do I know about the birth of our nation?" asked Ben. He reached for the door.

"Maybe I can help," said a deep voice.

Ben and Toby both jumped. They turned around.

"Oh! Hi, Big Ben," said Ben.

Ben's new neighbor sat on a chair by the trailer steps. He was named Ben too. Ben and his mom had started calling the man Big Ben.

It was a good name for him. He was heavyset. He looked big—even sitting down.

Big Ben's large head was bald on top. Gray and brown bushy hair grew in a circle around his head.

He wore small, wire-rimmed glasses. They had special glass at the bottom of each lens for reading. Big Ben looked very smart. Toby thought he must have a big brain in that big head.

"What are you doing?" Ben asked Big Ben.

"I'm thinking. And when I think, I like to keep my hands busy. So I'm shaping wood with this knife," Big Ben explained.

"What are you making?" asked Toby.

"A part for a machine that makes potato chips," Big Ben answered.

"But you can buy potato chips," said Toby.

"These are chips you can make at home. They are baked by the sun," said Big Ben. "I put a special spice on them. They have no fat. Here, try some. They're good for you." He held out a bowl of chips. Each boy took a few.

"These are good," said Ben. "Were these baked by the sun?"

"Yes," said Big Ben. "I baked them on top of the trailer. Now I'm making a box that will help the sun bake them even faster. I want them to be very crisp.

"I made this knife too. It has many blades. It will cut a potato very fast," Big Ben added.

"Big Ben is an inventor," Ben told Toby.

"Hey," said Toby, "maybe you could help me with my science project."

"Be glad to," said Big Ben. "And I'll help you, Ben, with your report. I know all there is to know about the birth of this country."

"Cool," said Ben. "I need three sources. I'll ask Miss Klug if you can be one of them."

"Both of you just let me know," said Big Ben. "I'm almost always here." He bent his head to work on his wood.

"Thanks, Big Ben," said Ben. He went into his trailer.

"Yeah, thanks," said Toby as he headed for his own trailer. Big Ben reminded him of someone. "Who?" he wondered.

15

Chapter 2

The Projects

The next afternoon, Big Ben finished the sun-powered potato chip maker. He was showing it to Ben and Toby after school. It was on the roof of his trailer. The boys took turns climbing the ladder to see it work.

"See," Big Ben said. "I just turn this key from down here. It makes all those

boards turn. That way the chips get the most sun. I can use the chip maker to dry fruit and other things too."

"Cool," said Toby. "This would make a great science fair project."

"Maybe you can think of something like it," said Big Ben. "There is a great deal of energy in nature. I once proved that lightning holds electric charges."

"Didn't Ben Franklin do that a long time ago?" asked Toby.

"Yes," Big Ben nodded. He gave Toby a knowing look. "The sun and wind also have great power. Think about that for a couple of days. Look around you. Come up with a problem. Then we'll figure it out together."

"OK, great," said Toby. "I'm going home. I'll see you after supper, Ben."

"Can't," replied Ben. "I have to go to the library. See you tomorrow."

As Toby walked away, Ben turned to Big Ben.

"Miss Klug says I can use you as one of my sources. But I have to go to the library for my other two. Mom's taking me after supper. Do you want to answer some questions now or after I go to the library?"

"What are the questions?" asked Big Ben.

"I guess I don't know what questions to ask," said Ben.

"You'd better go to the library first," said Big Ben. "Libraries are wonderful places. You can read

18

anything you want. I'll answer your questions when you're ready."

"It'll be too late tonight when I get back from the library," said Ben. "How about tomorrow afternoon?"

"Good idea. I don't want to stay up too late. Early to bed and early to rise, makes a man healthy, wealthy, and wise," said Big Ben. "I'll see you tomorrow."

Ben gave the man a funny look. Where had he heard that saying before?

The next morning, Toby and Ben stood by the entrance to the trailer park. They were waiting for the rest of the Koots.

"Does Big Ben remind you of anyone?" asked Toby.

19

"Yeah," said Ben. "He looks like Ben Franklin. And he talks like him too."

"Weird," said Toby.

"What's weird?" asked Ty as he and Abe walked up. Gabe got there at the same time, coming from the other way.

"Yeah, what's weird?" asked Gabe.

Toby answered. "Ben's new neighbor looks and acts like Ben Franklin."

"Who's Ben Franklin?" asked Abe. "Some movie star?"

"No. He helped begin the United States. Our class is learning about that right now," said Ben. "He lived a couple hundred years ago."

"So he'd be dead now," explained Ty.

"Long dead," said Gabe. "Hey! Maybe it's his ghost."

"He's no ghost!" said Ben. "He's a real person."

"Have you touched him?" asked Ty.

"No," said Ben. "Did you touch him, Toby?"

"I don't think so," answered Toby.

Gabe said, "Why don't we all go to your place after school, Ben. We can meet Ben Franklin. And I'll hold out my hand to shake. If we shake hands, we'll know he's for real."

"Cool idea, man!" said Toby.

During school, Ben had a little time to work on his report. Toby spent a few minutes thinking about a science fair project. But mostly, the Koots thought about meeting Ben Franklin's ghost.

21

Chapter 3

Meeting Big Ben

At last the school bell rang. The Koots met on the playground to walk to Ben's trailer.

Ty led the way. He walked backward. That way he could talk to all the Koots at once.

"Is this Ben guy scary looking?" he asked.

"No," said Ben. "He looks like your everyday person."

"How long have you known him?" asked Gabe.

"About a week," said Ben. "The Smiths just moved out. They had three little kids. They left the trailer in a mess. Ben moved in the next day. I think he's fixing up the place."

"Does he go to work?" asked Abe.

"No," said Ben. "He's an inventor. He stays in the trailer most of the time. He spends a lot of time thinking."

The Koots asked Ben questions all the way home.

The Koots finally reached Big Ben's trailer. The man wasn't sitting outside as usual.

"Now what?" asked Ben.

"Knock on his door," said Ty.

23

"What will I say?" asked Ben.

"Say you want him to meet your friends," answered Gabe.

"Oh, yeah," said Ben as he knocked on the door.

The door flew open and Big Ben stood there. Ben jumped back. All the Koots behind him jumped back too.

Big Ben really was big. And seeing him through the screen made him look like a ghost. He didn't look very happy either.

"Hi," said Ben.

"Hello, Ben," said Big Ben. "What do you want?"

"I just wanted you to meet my other friends. This is Ty. And this is Abe," Ben said, pointing toward Abe and Ty. "And this is Gabe."

Gabe held out his hand, but the
screen door stood in the way.

"Glad to meet you," said Big Ben. "I'm afraid I'm a little busy just now. See you later, Ben." He shut the door.

Ben turned around. "Well, what do you think?"

"Looks like Ben Franklin," said Ty.

"Looks like a ghost," said Abe.

"He wouldn't shake my hand," Gabe added. "I bet my hand would have gone right through his."

Toby and Ben just looked at each other.

"You guys are crazy," Toby said. "He's just a man."

Ben said, "Sure. I bet he's just busy inventing something."

Ben didn't look as sure as he sounded.

Chapter 4

The Door That Wouldn't Open

After supper, Big Ben knocked on Ben's door.

"Do you want to ask me those questions now?" he asked when Ben opened the door.

"Sure. Come in," said Ben.

"I'm sorry I couldn't invite your friends in," Big Ben said. "I was in the middle of something."

Ben looked at Big Ben. He looked at his hands and his face. The big man looked just like an everyday person.

"That's OK," Ben said.

Big Ben sat down in a chair. Ben had written five questions.

Big Ben answered each question better than the books Ben had read. Ben listened and wrote as fast as he could.

"How do you know so much?" asked Ben. "It's like you were there."

"I've always liked history," said Big Ben. "I have a good mind for facts. And I think it's important to know

about the past. It helps us handle the future."

Ben thought that made sense.

"That's all," said Ben. "Thanks a lot for your help."

"No problem," replied Big Ben.

Just then, Ben's mom came into the living room.

"I have to run to the store, Ben. I'll be back soon," she said.

"Could I ride along?" asked Big Ben. "I need to pick up a few things."

"Sure," said Ben's mom.

"I'll come too," said Ben. He ran to the car and jumped in the backseat.

Big Ben rode in front with Ben's mom. They talked the whole way there. Big Ben knew many interesting facts.

Ben's mom parked the car in the huge lot. Then the three walked to the big front door.

Big Ben was first. When he stepped in front of the door, it didn't open. He stepped back.

Ben's mom stepped in front of the door. It opened right up. Ben and Big Ben followed her into the store.

Ben wondered why the door wouldn't open for Big Ben. Was it because he really was a ghost?

31

Chapter 5

Looking for Clues

"And the door wouldn't open for him!" Ben told the Koots. It was Saturday morning. They were at Abe's place, watching cartoons.

"I told you he was a ghost!" said Gabe.

"Did you touch him?" asked Toby.

"No," said Ben. "I don't go around touching people."

"Well, somebody has to try to touch him," said Ty. "I think we should go over there right now."

"What if we touch him and he is a ghost?" asked Abe. "He might haunt us for the rest of our lives."

"I'm not touching him," said Toby.

"I'm not touching him either," said Ben.

"I tried once and he wouldn't shake hands. I guess I'm not touching him either," said Gabe.

They all looked at Ty since it had been his idea. "Not me," said Ty, shaking his head.

"Now what?" asked Ben.

"I still need a science project," said Toby. "I don't want to talk to him by myself. But you guys could come with me. Maybe we'll learn something."

The Koots agreed that they'd go see Big Ben together.

Chapter 6

Go Fly a Kite

Big Ben was sitting on the chair outside his trailer. He had a faraway look on his face.

"Hi, Big Ben," said Ben. "Remember my friends?"

"Sure," said Big Ben. "You guys seem to stick together. I used to have a group of friends like that. We did many good things."

Big Ben got that faraway look again. Then he looked at Toby.

"So, Toby," he said. "Have you thought of a science project?"

"I'm thinking about wind power," answered Toby. "Is there something that flies and makes power?"

"How about a kite?" asked Big Ben. "I'm great with kites. I can show you how we used to make them. The kite could turn a wheel that makes power."

"Great," said Toby. "I've never made a kite. How do you make one?"

Big Ben went into his trailer. He came back out with a newspaper, some string, some sticks, and a homemade reel.

35

"You make crossbars like this," he said. "You run strings around the ends of the bars. Then you fold the paper like this."

As he folded the paper, Big Ben looked at the front page. "I used to print a better newspaper than this one," he said.

Ben looked at him. "You were a printer too?"

"Sure," said Big Ben. "I've been a printer, and I've helped the country. Now I invent things and think about things."

Gabe gulped. "You sure sound like Ben Franklin," he whispered.

Big Ben looked at him. "Yes," he said. "Scary, isn't it?"

The Koots were very quiet as they watched Big Ben finish the kite.

"Now, Toby," he said, "you can fly the kite. Attach the string to a reel like this. See, it's also a wheel. Then when the kite flies, it pulls the string. That turns the wheel. You have power until your string runs out. You could run a small machine on this power. Think about that."

"Thank you, sir," said Toby. Big Ben handed him the kite and the little wheel.

"Anything else I can do for you boys?" he asked.

Nobody said anything. At last Ben said, "Can you tell us what life was like back in the 1700s?"

"Sure," said Big Ben. He sat down on the chair. Gabe and Ty sat on the trailer steps. Ben, Toby, and Abe sat on the ground in front of the big man.

Big Ben told story after story about the beginning of the United States of America. The Koots sat and listened. They heard stories of finding new land and fighting for freedom. They also heard stories of starting a new country and stories of kings and generals. Big Ben's stories were better than Saturday morning cartoons.

Chapter 7

Answers to the Puzzle

Later, the boys were in Ben's trailer.

"If he's not a ghost, what is he?" asked Ty.

"Maybe he's just a smart man who knows a lot," answered Ben. "I'd like to be that smart. I'd like to know a lot."

"What about the door at the grocery store?" asked Abe. "That was weird."

"Maybe the door just stuck for a minute," said Ben.

"He even talks funny," said Gabe. "He talks like he's from long ago."

"I don't think he's from around here," said Ben.

"So where is he from?" asked Toby. He peered out the window. Big Ben still sat in his chair. Toby could tell that Big Ben was thinking again. He had that faraway look.

"I don't know where he's from," said Ben. "Why don't you go ask him, Toby?"

Toby was getting hungry. It was time for lunch.

"I think I'll go home for lunch. Maybe I'll stop and talk to Big Ben on my way."

"I'm going too," said Abe. "Come to my place after lunch. My mom's baking cookies."

Gabe and Ty decided to go home for lunch too.

Ben stood at his door as the other Koots gathered around Big Ben. He couldn't hear what the big man said. But he saw how everyone walked away quickly.

After lunch, the Koots met at Abe's. Each boy had a couple of fresh sugar cookies.

"What did Big Ben tell you guys?" asked Ben.

Toby looked at him. "You're the one who knows about Ben Franklin. So maybe this will mean something to you.

"Big Ben said he was born in Boston. He lived in Philadelphia before he moved here. And he spent a few years in England and France." Then Toby added, "Scary, isn't it?"

"I don't know **that** much about Ben Franklin," said Ben. "Maybe we should go to the library."

"Saturday afternoon at the library?" asked Ty.

"If we want to find out the truth, we have to do some reading," said Ben.

Everybody agreed. They walked to the library.

A half hour later, the Koots sat around a table at the library. They had found three books about Ben Franklin.

"Here it is," said Ty. "This book says that Ben Franklin was born in Boston. He moved to Philadelphia. He spent time in England. And he worked for the United States in France during the Revolutionary War."

Ty shut the book and looked up. "Scary, isn't it?" he asked.

Chapter 8

More Puzzle Pieces

Ben decided to read more about Ben Franklin. He wanted to find something that would prove whether or not Big Ben was a ghost.

The rest of the Koots looked around the library.

Toby found the rack that held the CDs. He found some good music. Too bad he didn't have a CD player. Then he found a book on how to draw horses.

Abe looked through the videos. He chose two tapes. His family had a VCR. He would ask the Koots over to watch the movies.

Gabe found some books on race cars. They had great pictures.

Ty found some books on sports. They had great pictures too.

The boys all had library cards. Their class had visited the library recently. Everyone had gotten a card. So each Koot checked out something.

The Koots spent all Saturday afternoon at the library. As they walked home, Ben told everyone what he had learned.

"You know that group of friends Big Ben was talking about? If he is Ben Franklin's ghost, he was talking

46

about the Junto. That's what the group members called themselves. They started the first library, a college, and a fire company. They also started a hospital and lots more.

"Franklin invented a stove that stands in the middle of a room," Ben continued. "And he invented a lightning rod. It keeps houses from being hurt when lightning strikes.

"He also invented glasses like the ones Big Ben wears. They're called bifocals," Ben added.

"I got an idea while I was reading," Ben went on. "Ben Franklin invented all kinds of things. He was very smart. Do you think he figured out how to bring himself back from the dead?"

"Wow!" said the Koots.

"You might be right," said Toby. "Maybe he isn't a ghost. Maybe he's real. He just came alive again. I saw a movie like that. This man was frozen. Then, years later, he melted. He looked just like everyone else. Except his clothes were old."

"Big Ben's clothes do look old," said Abe.

"Let's go talk to him again," said Gabe. He looked at everybody. They didn't look like they agreed with his idea.

"Let's wait until tomorrow," said Abe. "I have movies we can watch."

"Good idea," said Ben. "We can be thinking about what we want to ask Big Ben."

Chapter 9

The Disappearance

Saturday night, the Kooties Club watched movies at Abe's. One of the movies was scary. The subject of Big Ben didn't come up. Toby, Gabe, and Ben ran home after the movies. They looked at Big Ben's trailer. It was dark.

Big Ben wasn't anywhere to be seen Sunday. But the Koots didn't notice. They were busy the whole day. The boys were at Gabe's playing Slap Jack and Come Up.

Every so often they'd talk about how to ask Big Ben if he was a ghost. They finally decided on a way to find out. One of them would just ask him. They drew straws. Ben lost.

All Sunday night, Ben thought about how he'd ask the question. All day Monday at school, he thought about it. He finally decided he'd just ask, "Big Ben, are you Ben Franklin?"

On Monday after school, the Koots went to Big Ben's trailer. It was empty. The chair wasn't outside. The potato chip machine wasn't on the roof. There was a "For Rent" sign in front of the trailer. Ben hadn't gotten a chance to ask his question.

Chapter 10

Scary, Isn't It?

Ben and the Koots went into Ben's trailer. Ben's mom was there.

"Where is Big Ben?" asked Ben.

"Oh, he went on to another job," said Ben's mom.

"What other job?" asked Ben. "He just moved in."

"No, honey," said Ben's mom. "He was just fixing up the trailer. The Smiths left it in a mess."

"I know," said Ben. "But I thought he lived there."

"Just while he worked on it," said his mom.

"Do you guys want to see the inside?" she asked. "It's really nice now. I have a key in case the manager isn't here to show the trailer."

"Sure," said all the Koots.

They walked across the way to Big Ben's trailer. Ben's mom unlocked the door and let them in.

The rooms had all been painted. The kitchen looked like new. But the best part was the living room. In the middle of the room sat a square, black stove.

"A Franklin stove!" shouted Ben. "I knew he was Ben Franklin!"

The Koots all nodded. Their eyes
were big. They looked at the stove
that Ben Franklin invented.

"What did you say?" asked Ben's mom. "His name is Ben Freeman. He fixes places up. When he is done with one, he moves on to another. He isn't Ben Franklin. He was pulling your leg."

"I don't think so," said Abe. "He never touched any of us."

Ben's mom smiled at Abe. "I mean he was joking with you. That reminds me, Ben. He left something for you."

Ben's mom and the Koots went back to Ben's trailer. Ben's mom handed her son a sheet of paper.

"This is a copy of the Declaration of Independence," she said. "Big Ben said maybe you could use it for your report."

The paper looked yellow with age. The words on it were handwritten. All the names at the bottom were signed in black ink. Except for one. In blue ink was the name *Ben Franklin*.

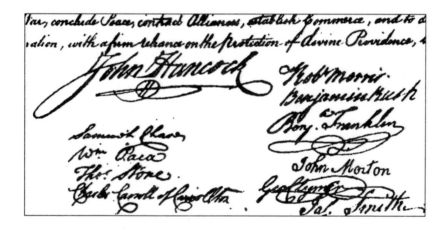

The Koots all stared at it.
"Scary, isn't it?" whispered Ty.
Ben's mom just laughed.
The Koots looked at each other.
Another mystery solved. Or was it?